"The doors of wisdom are never shut."

—*Benjamin Franklin*

"It isn't where you came from;

it's where you're going that counts."

—*Ella Fitzgerald*

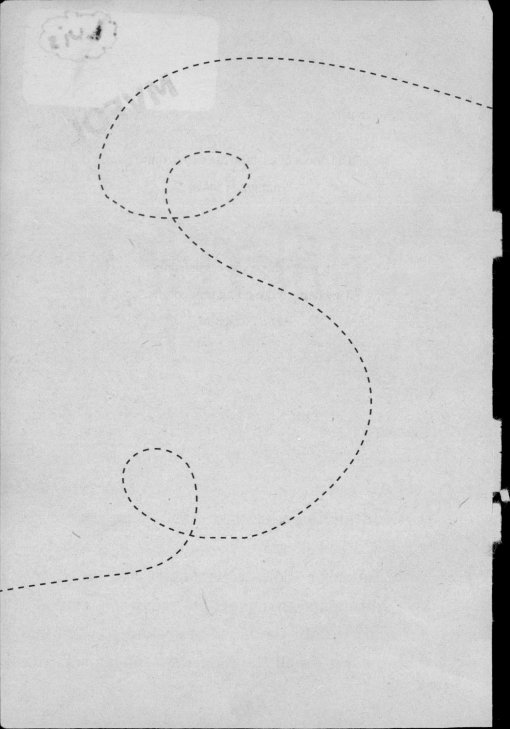

CHAPTER 1

Thwak.

Thwak.

Thwak.

How many times had Jake Everdale punched his new baseball glove? A hundred? A thousand? He didn't know, and he didn't care. He'd keep hitting and thumping and squashing and squishing it until the brand-new glove was as broken-down—in all the right ways—as his old one. Jake was pretty sure that the stiff leather had finally started to give, which made him even more determined to keep at it. That's why he was punching it in rhythm to his steps as he walked to school with his best friend, Emerson Lewis. The school day hadn't even started yet, but Jake was already daydreaming about baseball practice that afternoon.

Thwak.

"You think Coach will let me pitch today?" Jake asked.

Thwak.

"Maybe," Emerson replied. "He keeps putting you on third base, though. And third base is pretty important."

Thwak.

A slight frown crossed Emerson's face as he glanced over at Jake's glove. "Why'd you get a new glove anyway?" he continued. "Your old one was perfect."

Jake didn't answer right away. He didn't want

to lie to Emerson, but he couldn't exactly tell the whole truth: A mini-figure of Sir Isaac Newton had come to life to help Jake with his science project, and ripped up Jake's glove for one of his experiments.

It had all started when Jake made a wish at the old storm drain behind Franklin Elementary School. The kids called it the Wishing Well. According to legend, if you threw your most special belonging into the well, your wish would be granted.

Jake had been struggling in school for as long as he could remember, and it had gotten so bad that Mom and Dad were going to take away baseball if he didn't get a good grade on his science project. Jake thought the Wishing Well was his only hope, but he couldn't bear to give up his baseball card collection.

Instead, Jake threw in his Heroes of History action figures. Jake hoped that they were special enough since they'd been a gift from his aunt

Margaret, who was the best neuroscientist in the world. But when the Wishing Well brought Sir Isaac and famous pilot Amelia Earhart to life, it almost caused more problems than it solved!

"I had some money saved up," Jake finally said. It wasn't really an answer to Emerson's question, but by then they had reached school, and Emerson was distracted.

"Better put your glove away before Ms. Turner sees it," Emerson told Jake as they entered the classroom. Jake wasn't really listening, though. His attention had been captured by the box on Ms. Turner's desk. It was glittering gold, with bright red question marks glued to the sides. Jake immediately wondered why it was there—and what was in it.

"Check it out," Jake said, gesturing to the box.

"That's new," Emerson replied. "Do you know what it is?"

Jake shrugged. "I don't have a clue."

"Tell us something we don't know, Ever*fail*."

Jake didn't need to turn around to know who was speaking. Only Aiden Allen, the class know-it-all, called him Everfail instead of Everdale. It was no secret that Jake struggled in school—a lot. But nobody else seemed to enjoy his difficulty as much as Aiden did. Jake didn't understand why Aiden hated him so much. Aiden was a great student. He could get all As in his sleep.

Jake could feel that familiar, uncomfortable redness creeping into his neck. He wished he had something to say—something that would make Aiden shut up for a change. But, like always, Jake was totally tongue-tied when Aiden started mocking him in front of everybody.

"I know *exactly* what's in that box," Aiden said loudly. "Doesn't anybody remember what's coming up?"

"You want to tell us or not?" Emerson asked.

Aiden paused for a long moment. "It's for Living History Night, of course," he announced.

The other kids started chattering excitedly.

Living History Night was a big deal for the whole school—but *especially* for the fourth grade. Every year, each student was assigned an important person from history to research. They had to make a costume, find props, and prepare a first-person biographical speech. Then, on a special night, they had to give a presentation to the whole school—including all the teachers, their parents, and the principal!

"I hope I get Marie Curie," Hannah said excitedly. "She was the coolest scientist ever. She discovered radioactivity!"

"Where would Spider-Man be without her?" Jake joked. "I hope I get a baseball player. I already have a uniform, so my costume would be all set."

"A baseball player?" Aiden sneered. "Yeah, that sounds about your speed. But baseball doesn't really have anything to do with history."

"Are you kidding?" Emerson spoke up. "What about Jackie Robinson? Not only was he one of the greatest ballplayers in history, he ended segregation in baseball *and* he was a soldier during World War Two!"

Aiden ignored him.

"I know who I want," he said, speaking over Emerson. "Benjamin Franklin. My brother was Franklin three years ago, so I already have the wig. And I even have a *real* copy of the Constitution on *real* parchment. It looks *really* old and official."

Good for you, Jake thought. He glanced at the portrait of Benjamin Franklin that hung over Ms. Turner's desk. Ben Franklin was smiling slightly, like he knew a secret. He looked like a pretty nice guy, actually . . . the exact opposite of Aiden.

"Don't you think I'd be the *perfect* Franklin?" Aiden continued.

"I guess." Hannah shrugged. "It's a lot of work, though. You don't just have to do your own project—you have to be in charge of the whole show. You'd be, like, the host."

"You think I don't know that?" Aiden asked.

"It's the most important role in the whole show. Ms. Turner has probably already picked the person who gets to be Franklin. I just hope it's me."

"But it's a random drawing," Jake pointed out.

Aiden gave him a withering look. "Do you *really* think Ms. Turner is going to leave something so important up to chance?" he asked. "A lousy Franklin will make the whole night a giant fail."

Just then, Ms. Turner entered the room, right as the bell rang.

"Glove!" Emerson reminded Jake.

Jake shoved his baseball glove in his backpack as all the students scurried to their seats. From the middle of the front row, Jake had a better view of the mysterious box than anybody.

"Good morning, class!" Ms. Turner said.

"Good morning," everyone replied.

A smile crossed Ms. Turner's face as she picked up the box. "I'm sure you're all wondering what's in here," she began.

Jake could imagine Aiden's hand shooting into the air behind him. Sure enough, Ms. Turner called on him.

"Is it names for Living History Night?" Aiden asked.

"That's right!" Ms. Turner replied. "For the last four years, you've all watched Living History Night from the audience. At last, it's your time to shine!"

Jake glanced out the window. It was a perfect day, with bright sunshine and a gentle breeze blowing puffy white clouds across the sky. Jake's thoughts drifted back to baseball practice later that afternoon. He could almost feel the metal bat in his hands and the sun glinting off his batting helmet.

Ms. Turner was still talking, though, so Jake tried to pay attention.

"A few rules," she was saying. "You will pick one name, and one name only. No do-overs, no trades, no swaps, no special requests. Got it?"

"Got it," the class replied in unison.

"And, of course, the student who pulls Benjamin Franklin will have a few extra responsibilities," Ms. Turner continued. "Now, I have written copies of the instructions here. Don't forget to take one when you choose your name. Elizabeth!"

Jake straightened in his seat. Ms. Turner was starting with the front row—which meant in just a moment, he'd be choosing a name from the box.

Elizabeth seemed pleased with her pick. Her curls bounced as she bounded back to her seat.

"Marco," Ms. Turner said.

Jake's turn was next. His heart was hammering and his palms were all sweaty. It was almost as nerve-racking as going up to bat with the bases loaded.

Almost.

"Jake!"

Jake stood up and walked to Ms. Turner's desk. He closed his eyes and reached into the box. The slips of paper rustled under his fingertips, as if they were trying to whisper the names written on them.

Please Jackie Robinson. Please Babe Ruth. Please Hank Aaron, Jake thought as he chose one of the slips. He didn't even realize he was holding his breath as he unfolded the scrap of paper.

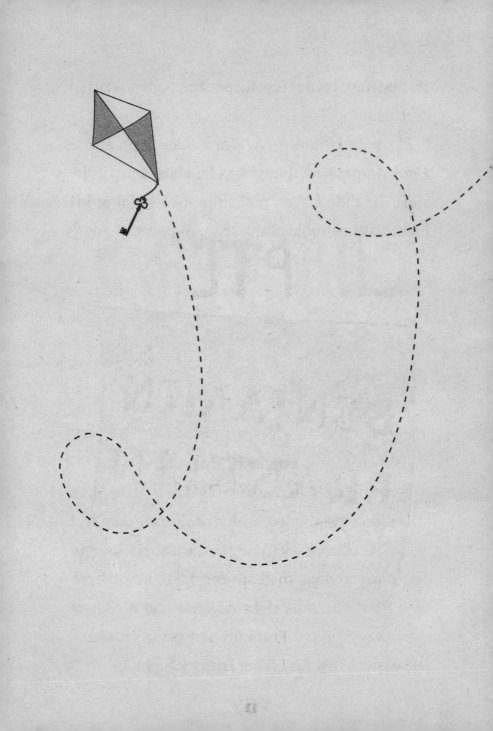

CHAPTER 2

"No!" Jake yelped.

"Is there a problem, Jake?" Ms. Turner asked.

"Yes! I mean—no!" Jake replied in a panic. The other students giggled, which only made Jake feel worse. He slunk back to his seat, wishing he could bolt out the door instead. But Jake didn't have time for daydreams right now. He had to figure out a way to ditch Franklin and get a smaller— and easier—role for Living History Night.

Ms. Turner knows how important the Franklin role is, he reminded himself. *She doesn't want Living History Night to be a disaster. There's no way she'll let the worst student have the most important role.*

Jake's hand shot into the air.

"Yes, Jake?" Ms. Turner said.

Jake hurried up to her desk. "Ms. Turner, there was a big mistake," he whispered. "I accidentally pulled Franklin."

He held out the slip of paper, but Ms. Turner didn't even glance at it. "Did you!" she exclaimed, all too cheerfully. "Congratulations, Jake! I know you'll be an excellent Benjamin Franklin."

Jake blinked. "But—" he faltered. "But I heard that the person who plays Franklin is specially chosen," Jake continued. "Just to make sure that they'll do a great job. And, you know, Aiden really, *really* wants it. And he's amazing at, like, everything. We could just trade and—"

Ms. Turner held up her hand. "Let me stop you right there," she said. "We've never assigned the role of Franklin, so that rumor is officially untrue."

Great, Jake thought. *The one time in his whole life Aiden has the wrong answer.*

"Jake, I think you're going to be an *excellent* Franklin," Ms. Turner said. "Will it be challenging? Sure. But I think—no, I *know*—that you're up for it."

Jake tried to manage a smile. He wished he could be as confident as Ms. Turner.

"Plus, the student who plays Franklin has the opportunity to earn extra credit," Ms. Turner continued. "I know you've asked about that before. Here you go—there's more information in this special handout."

From the way Ms. Turner handed Jake the extra assignment, Jake could tell the conversation was over.

Jake's day only got worse from there. There were Tater Tots at lunch, but Jake could barely enjoy them as everyone chatted excitedly about their historical figures. Aiden was going on and on about his pick—Napoleon Bonaparte—as if he'd never wanted to choose Franklin. Emerson had lucked out and picked Jackie Robinson! Jake was happy for his best friend—and a little jealous. Picking a ballplayer for Living History Night was like hitting a homework home run.

"What about you, Jake?" Hannah asked. "Who did you get?"

Everyone at the lunch table turned to look at him.

Jake swallowed unexpectedly; a half-chewed Tater Tot got stuck in his throat and made him start coughing. Emerson whacked him on the back a couple times. That only made *more* people stare.

"Franklin," Jake finally choked out. "I got Franklin."

For a moment, nobody said anything.

"Whoa," Sebastian said.

"That's great!" Hannah said loudly. "You're going to be a great Franklin. In fact—"

A loud, mean laugh interrupted her. It sounded like a cross between a sick seal and a truck backfiring.

"Look at the bright side, Jake," Aiden announced. "No matter how bad you fail, it's only one night. It will just live in everyone's memories *forever.*"

After baseball practice, Jake went right home to get started on his project. But how?

Jake glanced over at the dollhouse in the corner of his room. Technically, it belonged to his little sister, Julia. But as soon as she'd met the miniature Sir Isaac, she'd insisted on moving it into Jake's room. Sir Isaac and Miss Earhart had been gone for a couple of weeks now. It was clear they weren't coming back.

But Julia hadn't taken the dollhouse back to her own room. And whenever Jake thought about Sir

Isaac and Miss Earhart, he didn't want her to . . . just in case.

Jake rummaged around in his backpack until he found the Living History Night assignment, including the extra information for his Benjamin Franklin role.

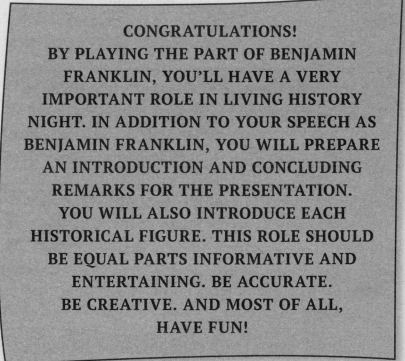

CONGRATULATIONS!
BY PLAYING THE PART OF BENJAMIN FRANKLIN, YOU'LL HAVE A VERY IMPORTANT ROLE IN LIVING HISTORY NIGHT. IN ADDITION TO YOUR SPEECH AS BENJAMIN FRANKLIN, YOU WILL PREPARE AN INTRODUCTION AND CONCLUDING REMARKS FOR THE PRESENTATION. YOU WILL ALSO INTRODUCE EACH HISTORICAL FIGURE. THIS ROLE SHOULD BE EQUAL PARTS INFORMATIVE AND ENTERTAINING. BE ACCURATE. BE CREATIVE. AND MOST OF ALL, HAVE FUN!

Have fun? Jake wondered incredulously. Was Ms. Turner trying to be funny?

Jake read over the instructions again, then shook his head in dismay. There was no way he could pull it off. The project was way too hard—way too much work—way too much pressure—

Jake didn't even know where to begin.

Well, actually . . . maybe he did know where to begin.

Jake glanced back at the dollhouse. Would the Wishing Well grant his next wish—or was it one and done?

There was only one way to find out.

Jake took a deep breath and grabbed onto the edge of his desk so tightly that his knuckles turned white.

"I wish . . ." he whispered, "I wish for extra help."

POP!

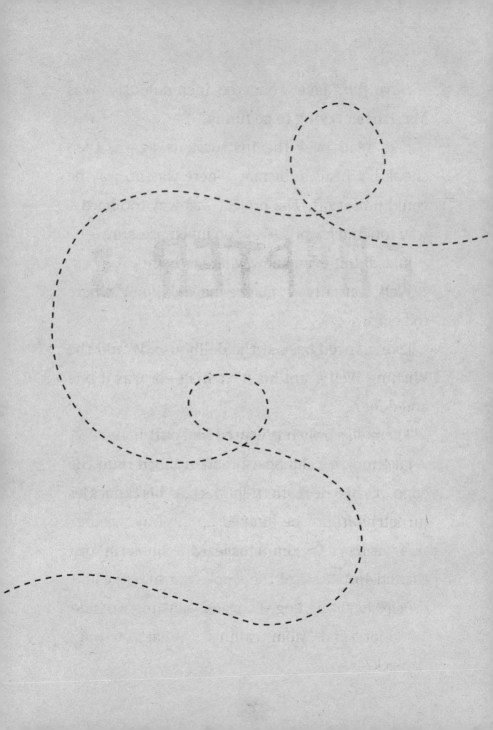

CHAPTER 3

Jake should've been prepared for what happened
next: the small but scary explosion, the sudden
cloud of smoke, the fiery sparks that blazed without burning. But he jumped up anyway, waving
his arms like a windmill to clear the smoke before
it could waft toward the smoke alarm. He could
already hear his dog, Flapjack, howling outside
the door, and Mom calling, "What's wrong,
Flapjack?"

Jake stared at his desk, transfixed, as the smoke began to clear. There was a tiny person, just three inches tall, standing on the Living History Night assignment. Even through the haze, Jake could tell that she was all dressed up in a long velvet gown, with a fancy stole wrapped around her shoulders. Her glossy black hair was swept back in an elegant style. Long strands of moonlight-colored pearls were draped around her neck, the perfect complement to her dark skin. The woman glanced from side to side, a bright curiosity lighting up her eyes.

"Now I *know* I'm supposed to enter stage left," she said, almost to herself, "but I've never seen a backstage as cluttered as this one."

"H-hello," Jake said. "I'm—I'm Jake."

The woman peered up at him. If she was alarmed at the sight of a giant boy who towered over her, she didn't show it.

"Well, hello, young man!" the woman said in a voice that was as elegant as her outfit. "I'm Ella Fitzgerald and it is a *pleasure* to meet you."

Ella Fitzgerald, Ella Fitzgerald, Ella Fitzgerald, Jake silently repeated the name to himself. It was kind of familiar, but he couldn't remember where he'd heard it before. It seemed rude to ask Ms. Fitzgerald outright, so Jake snuck a glance at the brochure that had come with his Heroes of History figurines.

Ella Fitzgerald
1917–1996, United States
This Hero of History was known as the "First Lady of Song" for her incredible voice and contributions to the field of music.

"You must have been born into a theater family," Ms. Fitzgerald said. "Young stage-hands such as yourself have the performing arts running in their blood. Are your parents musicians? Actors? Or are they behind-the-scenes folks?"

"Uh . . ." Jake paused. His thoughts were

swirling more wildly than a tornado, and he couldn't figure out which one to focus on first. Ms. Fitzgerald seemed ready to perform onstage . . . and she thought that Jake worked in a theater . . .

But most of all, Jake couldn't figure out why Ella Fitzgerald, a famous singer, had been sent to help him with his Living History Night project. Did the Wishing Well—or whatever was in charge—think he was going to put on some kind of Benjamin Franklin–themed song and dance? The answer to that question was absolutely, positively, no way, *never*! Jake's voice was so bad he didn't even sing in the shower.

"Young man?" Ms. Fitzgerald said, raising an eyebrow. "Are you all right?"

"Errr . . ." Jake said. He had to think fast—and hope he said the right thing. "I'm sorry, Ms. Fitzgerald, but . . . well . . . the concert has been canceled."

Jake bit his lower lip, worried that Ms. Fitzgerald would throw a diva-sized fit. But to his surprise, she threw back her head and laughed.

"Canceled? That's ridiculous," Ms. Fitzgerald replied. "Everyone knows that the show must go on—no matter what."

"But . . . it can't," Jake said helplessly.

Ms. Fitzgerald, however, wouldn't budge. "Young man, I must insist," she said. Her voice was polite but firm. "I know for a fact that it's a sold-out show. The house must be packed. I'm all warmed up and ready to go!"

Ms. Fitzgerald started to sway in time to music that only she could hear. She snapped her fingers as a smile spread across her face. Then she opened her mouth and started to sing a bunch of quick, bright sounds—"*Doot-n-du-du-du-de-dow-dah*"—snapping her fingers to the jazzy beat.

Jake was completely captivated by the spontaneous performance from one of the greatest singers of all time. He didn't notice that he was tapping his foot along. He didn't even notice the change in Flapjack's barking . . . or the knock at the door . . . or the creaky hinges as his bedroom door swung open.

But Jake *did* notice when there was a loud *crash* in the doorway. He turned around just in time to see Emerson standing there, a look of pure shock on his face and a pile of books scattered on the floor around his feet.

CHAPTER 4

Jake stood up so fast that his chair toppled over. "Emerson!" he exclaimed. "When—what—"

Emerson's eyes were wider than Jake had ever seen them. "Is that *Ella Fitzgerald*?" he gasped.

Jake scrambled over to Emerson, pulled him into the room, and slammed the door. "Listen," Jake began in a panic. "You have to *swear* that you won't—"

"I can't believe this!" In his excitement,

Emerson was practically yelling. "Lady Ella! The First Lady of Song! The Queen of Jazz!"

Ms. Fitzgerald chuckled as she acknowledged Emerson with a slight curtsy. "The pleasure is all mine, young man," she said. "What's your name?"

"I'm Emerson! Lewis! I mean, Emerson Lewis," he replied, crouching on his knees to get a better look at the miniature singer. Then he glanced back at Jake in astonishment. "Is she for real?" he asked. "Like, really real? Why is she so small?"

"Shhh!" Jake tried to hush his friend. "She can hear you, you know. And so can the rest of the world. Would you *please* lower your voice?"

"Excuse me!" Ms. Fitzgerald's voice rang out. "If you could just point me in the direction of the stage . . ."

"Sorry," Jake apologized. "There's been . . . uh . . . an unavoidable, ah, delay . . ."

Ms. Fitzgerald frowned.

"But if you'd like to wait in the green room,"

Emerson suddenly spoke up as he gestured to Julia's dollhouse, "I'm sure we can straighten everything out."

"Thank you, Emerson," Ms. Fitzgerald said in a dignified voice as she entered Julia's deluxe dollhouse.

Jake stared at Emerson in astonishment. How had he known just what to say to Ms. Fitzgerald? And perhaps more important . . .

"How do you know so much about Ella Fitzgerald?" Jake asked.

From the dollhouse, the boys could hear Ms. Fitzgerald warming up her voice. *"Shu-bu-sku-ba-du-dwee-zee-dee!"*

"Lady Ella, *scatting*," Emerson marveled. "I can't believe it."

"Scatting?" Jake asked. "What's that?"

"It's like musical improv, and it's really, really hard to do—even for the best jazz singers," Emerson explained. "The way she's singing—that's not a song that exists, you know. Ms.

Fitzgerald is just inventing it, right here, right now, in real time! And we get to listen!"

"Wow," Jake said. "That's pretty cool."

"Understatement of the year," Emerson said. "Jake. Buddy. Tell me *everything*."

Jake glanced over his shoulder at the dollhouse. Since Ms. Fitzgerald was completely engrossed in her song, he pulled Emerson over to the far corner of his room.

"If I tell you . . ." Jake began slowly, "then you have to *promise* me you won't tell anybody else."

"Sure, I promise," Emerson said. "But why are you so upset? This is the coolest—craziest—most incredible thing ever!"

Easy for you to say, Jake thought—but he realized he wasn't being very fair to Emerson. After all, Emerson had no idea what Sir Isaac and Miss Earhart had put him through.

"Before the science fair, I made a wish at the

Wishing Well," Jake explained. "I wished for extra help, and I threw in my Heroes of History—"

Emerson made a face. "The Heroes of History set was your most special belonging?"

"Of course not," Jake said. "But the point is, two of them came to life to help with my science project."

It took a moment or two for Emerson to grasp exactly what Jake meant. "But . . ." he began. "You . . . you won a ribbon. Second place."

"It's not like that," Jake rushed to explain. "I didn't cheat. Believe me, they were way more trouble than help. But they did inspire me . . . and point me in the right direction. The project was all my own work. I promise. I'm not a cheater."

"I know," Emerson said—a little too quickly. "I didn't call you a cheater."

"Anyway," Jake said, "I wished for help with Living History Night and—*poof!* Ms. Fitzgerald showed up."

When Emerson didn't reply, Jake started talking really fast. "You don't understand, Emerson; you wouldn't believe how much work it is," he said in a rush. "I mean, *Benjamin Franklin*? I don't want to fail up there, in front of the whole school!"

"I do understand," Emerson argued. "That's why I came over. I brought you a bunch of my dad's history books. To help you get started."

Jake glanced over at the door, where the books Emerson had brought were still scattered across the floor. A rush of gratitude surged through him. "Thank you," he said. "You're a great friend."

"Bop-buh-bah-bah-dah-deet-n-dee!"

Both boys glanced over at the dollhouse.

"Man. Ella Fitzgerald," Emerson marveled. "Did you know she has perfect pitch? And she never took a single music lesson—not even one?"

Jake shook his head. "How did you know that?" he asked.

"My dad, of course," Emerson replied. "He's, like, her number-one fan."

That made sense, Jake realized. After all, Emerson's dad taught music at the high school. He even played in a local jazz band on the weekends. "Maybe that's why Ms. Fitzgerald looked kind of familiar to me," he said.

"My dad owns every single one of her albums," Emerson said. "Want to come over and listen to her songs?"

"That would be great," Jake replied. "I still haven't figured out why Ella Fitzgerald appeared. I mean, a scientist for the science fair—that made sense. And Miss Earhart inspired me to research the science of flight. But I can't figure out a connection between Ella Fitzgerald and Benjamin Franklin."

Emerson shrugged. "I don't know, either," he said. "Maybe listening to her music will help."

"Actually . . ." Jake began, "I should probably stay here. I shouldn't leave Ms. Fitzgerald alone."

"Just bring her," Emerson said.

"I don't think that's such a good idea," Jake tried to tell him. "Trust me on this."

But Emerson had already walked over to the dollhouse. "Ms. Fitzgerald?" he called. "Would you be available for a sound check?"

A few minutes later, Jake and Emerson arrived at Emerson's house. Mrs. Lewis was blasting some cool African music while she worked on a project for the Wonderland Stage, where she was the artistic director.

"Hey, Mrs. Lewis," Jake said.

Mrs. Lewis looked up from her notebook and smiled. "Hello, Mr. Franklin," she replied. "Congratulations, Jake! Emerson told me about your big role at Living History Night."

Jake smiled weakly.

"Mom, can we hang out in Dad's studio for a little while?" Emerson asked. "Jake wants to listen to some Ella Fitzgerald songs. He's never heard her music before."

Mrs. Lewis clutched her chest and pretended to stagger backwards. "Be still my heart!" she cried. "*Never* heard Lady Ella? *'A-tisket, a-tasket, la la la la la . . .'*"

"*Mom*. Stop," Emerson groaned as Mrs. Lewis danced around the table, humming. But Jake was grinning. With her big personality and even bigger heart, Mrs. Lewis was one of his favorite people on the planet. No matter what was wrong, it didn't seem quite so bad when she was around.

"Only Lady Ella could turn a nursery rhyme into a hit song," Mrs. Lewis continued, like she didn't even realize that Emerson was dying of embarrassment. "Jake, you are in for a treat. Go ahead, boys, but remember to be respectful of Daddy's space, E."

"We will," Emerson promised. Then he led Jake through the house to a small room in the back, where Mr. Lewis kept all of his instruments. There was a trombone and a tuba, a steel drum, and a range of cool percussion instruments mounted on the wall. The opposite wall had framed sheet music on display, along with photographs of famous jazz musicians. Jake didn't know where to look first.

Suddenly, Jake realized that his backpack was rustling. "Sorry, Ms. Fitzgerald," he said quickly as he opened it up and helped her climb out. "Emerson's dad loves jazz, too. This is his music room."

"Why, he sounds like a friend I just haven't met yet," Ella declared. She peered up at the wall of photos. "What do we have here! Chick Webb, Dizzy Gillespie, Louis Armstrong, Billie Holiday. That's a real rogues' gallery you've got!"

Jake and Emerson must've looked confused, because Ms. Fitzgerald started to laugh. "It's a joke, boys," she explained. "I've had the good fortune to perform with those fine musicians—and the even better fortune to count them as friends."

"My dad collects autographed albums of famous jazz musicians," Emerson told her. "He's been hoping to add one of yours to his collection for a while now."

Ms. Fitzgerald looked pleased. "Is that a fact?" she said.

Emerson leaned closer to Jake and said in a low voice, "I tried to get one for Father's Day last year. But it cost a thousand dollars!"

"Are you kidding?" Jake asked.

"I wish," Emerson said. Then he opened a cupboard. "Check out this old record player," he told Jake. "My dad found it at a garage sale and spent a whole year fixing it up. He likes listening to old records better than MP3s."

Emerson plucked a record from the shelf and carefully slid it out of the protective sleeve.

"Why, that's one of my records!" Ms. Fitzgerald said. "*Lullabies of Birdland,* a personal favorite."

Emerson placed the shiny black record onto the player and carefully aligned the needle with one of the grooves. The speakers crackled; then the music washed over Jake, and he closed his eyes to listen. There were bright horns and a catchy beat, a piano tinkling an upbeat melody, and then—

Ella Fitzgerald, the one and only Ella Fitzgerald, started to sing. Her voice was like nothing Jake had ever heard before, rich and resonant, joyfully belting out notes high and low.

As the song came to an end, Jake realized that Ms. Fitzgerald had been singing along to the recording. He and Emerson burst into applause.

"Wow," Jake marveled. "That was incredible!"

Ms. Fitzgerald clasped her hands behind her back and bowed. "Thank you. Thank you very much," she said. Then she turned to Emerson. "I have a little surprise for your father."

Jake and Emerson leaned forward to take a closer look as Ms. Fitzgerald proudly showed them the album cover. There, on the corner, in tiny, looping letters, was her signature: *Ella Fitzgerald.*

"Now his autograph collection will be complete," Ms. Fitzgerald said.

It took Jake a moment to understand. Ms. Fitzgerald had autographed one of Mr. Lewis's records! *Is that worth a thousand dollars now?* he wondered. Jake was about to ask Emerson when he caught a glimpse of Emerson's face. It was stuck somewhere between shock and horror as Emerson, unblinking, stared at the album cover.

"What . . . did . . . you . . . do?" he asked slowly. "Oh no! This is terrible—"

"Excuse us," Jake said to Ms. Fitzgerald. Then he grabbed Emerson's sleeve and dragged him into the hallway.

"Pull it together!" Jake said. "She didn't mean—"

"Don't you get it?" Emerson howled. "This is a *huge* disaster! She defaced one of my dad's favorite albums, and he's gonna think it was *me*, and Mom already warned me to be respectful of his stuff! He's going to be *so mad—*"

"Maybe he won't notice," Jake said hopefully.

Emerson shot him a dirty look. "Won't notice? Are you kidding? He loves his record collection. Believe me, he'll notice."

"Well . . ." Jake said, "she was only trying to help. I think you should apologize."

"Are you kidding? *She* should apologize!" Emerson said hotly.

Jake's temper started to rise, too. "This is what I tried to warn you about—but you wouldn't listen," he snapped. "You think it's so cool to have these tiny geniuses running around, but *news flash*—they're *real,* they're not toys, and they get into all kinds of trouble and you can't control them!"

"Then maybe you shouldn't have brought her here!" Emerson yelled. "Maybe you should've just stayed home!"

"Yeah, maybe I should've!" Jake yelled back.

"Well, you know the way out!" Emerson shouted.

Jake didn't say another word as he marched back into Mr. Lewis's music studio and opened up his backpack. "Come on, Ms. Fitzgerald," he said. "We're leaving."

Ms. Fitzgerald's eyes were wide with worry as she hurried into Jake's backpack. "I didn't—" she began.

"I know. It's okay," Jake said. "We can talk about it later."

As soon as Ms. Fitzgerald was safely stashed in the backpack, Jake stormed out. Was it his imagination, or did Emerson already look like he was feeling sorry?

Jake didn't care. He left without saying another word.

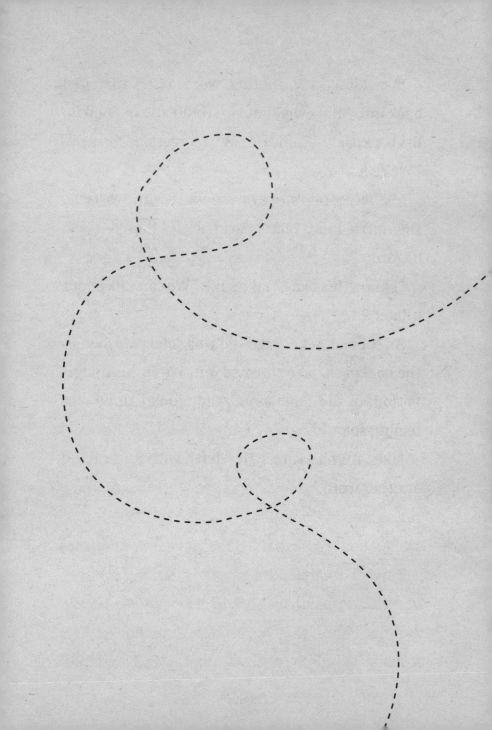

CHAPTER 5

Jake's fight with Emerson left a gaping hole in his life. Walking to school alone, eating lunch at different tables, sitting at opposite ends of the bench during batting practice . . . nothing seemed normal without Emerson around. Jake and Emerson had never really had a big fight before, so Jake wasn't sure what he should do next. He had a sinking feeling that he needed to apologize. He probably should've been watching Ms. Fitzgerald more closely. After all, Jake had learned the hard way just what could go wrong with Sir Isaac and Miss Earhart. It wasn't Emerson's fault that he didn't understand.

But whenever Jake decided to tell Emerson that he was sorry, he remembered how angry Emerson had been. Maybe Emerson didn't want an apology from Jake.

Maybe he didn't even want to be friends anymore.

Jake pushed the thought from his mind and reached for Mr. Lewis's Franklin books. They tugged at his conscience, a constant reminder of what a good friend Emerson was—and how much Jake missed him. At the same time, though, Jake knew that he had to get started on his Living History Night project. If he'd learned anything from the science fair, it was that waiting until the last minute was almost always a recipe for disaster. But as the days passed, Jake was painfully aware that he was falling behind. He'd made a good start on his stack of note cards with cool facts about Ben Franklin, but he needed a costume, and props, and introductions for all the other historical figures, too.

Jake flipped through one of the books, then glanced out the window. It was a teacher workday, so all the students had a special day off from school. But it didn't feel like a day off for Jake, not with Living History Night looming over his head. If he and Emerson hadn't had that big fight, maybe they would've been working on their projects together. Maybe they would've been taking a break right about now, and heading into the backyard to play catch.

"Penny for your thoughts?" Ms. Fitzgerald's voice drifted to him from the dollhouse.

"Huh?" Jake asked.

"It's an expression," she explained. "It means, what are you thinking about? Or, what's wrong?"

Jake didn't want to talk about the fight with Emerson. Instead, he decided to tell Ms. Fitzgerald about his assignment. "It's a big project for school," he began. "I have to give a presentation as Benjamin Franklin. With a costume and props and everything. *And* introduce all the other presenters. I'll be onstage the whole time."

Ms. Fitzgerald's eyes brightened. "Why, Jake! You'll be the star of the show!" she declared.

"That's the problem!" Jake groaned as he buried his head in his hands. "I don't *want* to be the star. I don't even want to be in the show at all. But I don't have a choice."

"Maybe I can help," Ms. Fitzgerald said.

Jake perked up a little. He hadn't been able to figure out how one of the greatest jazz singers of all time could help him with a Benjamin Franklin project, but maybe Ms. Fitzgerald would know what to do.

Jake scrounged around in the mess on his desk until he found the special instructions for his role as Franklin. "This is the assignment," he told her. "If you have any ideas, I'd love to hear them."

"Oh, I know a thing or two about show business," Ms. Fitzgerald assured him. "Lady Ella will do right by you, Jake. Don't you worry about a thing."

For the first time, Jake let himself feel a little hopeful. He had to trust that the Wishing Well had sent him just the right helper, even if he didn't quite understand. After all, Sir Isaac and Miss Earhart had inspired the science project that had earned him a second-place ribbon and an A minus.

"Jake!" Mom called. "Flapjack needs to go out."

"On my way," Jake replied. He was grateful to have a reason to escape from his bedroom and the mountain of work on his desk. And maybe by the time Jake got back, Ms. Fitzgerald would have a whole list of ideas for him.

Taking Flapjack for a walk was just what Jake needed. It felt so good to be outside, in the beautiful sunshine. There was a baseball game after school the next day, and Jake was already counting down the hours. On the field, he'd be completely focused on the game—a much-needed brain break from the Living History project . . .

Suddenly, Flapjack tugged at his leash and started to whine, yanking Jake out of his baseball daydream. Jake stopped, too, and looked around.

He'd walked right to Emerson's house—as if he were on autopilot.

"Come on, Flapjack," Jake said urgently, nudging his dog along. If Emerson glanced outside and saw Jake lingering on the sidewalk like a weirdo, what would he think?

Jake didn't want to run the risk of ambling past Emerson's house again, so he and Flapjack took the long way home. Almost an hour had passed by the time Jake was climbing the stairs back to his room. Right away, he noticed that something wasn't right. His bedroom door was ajar, and Jake was certain—well, almost certain—that he'd closed it before he left.

He *had* closed it, right?

Suddenly, Jake wasn't so sure.

If Ms. Fitzgerald had left the room and was wandering around the house somewhere . . . or if Mom had gone in to put away laundry . . .

Then Jake heard it: the unmistakable sound of breaking glass.

Jake's palms were suddenly very sweaty. He slowly pushed open the door, wondering what he would find.

Ms. Fitzgerald wasn't alone anymore.

In fact, she was singing a duet with Jake's little sister!

"Julia!" Jake yelled as loud as he dared. "You know you're not supposed to go in my room without asking!"

The song stopped abruptly as Ms. Fitzgerald and Julia turned to Jake. It was obvious that Julia had raided Mom's closet in an attempt to dress like Ms. Fitzgerald. She was wobbling around the room in a pair of too-big high heels, trailing Mom's long bathrobe behind her. Julia had even wrapped a feather boa around her shoulders and was warbling into a hairbrush like it was a pretend microphone.

Julia took a few shaky steps toward Jake, holding the edge of the desk for support. She made a face. "Wet, yuck," she said.

"What do you mean, *wet*?" Jake asked suspiciously.

That's when Jake noticed that his glass of water had shattered, leaving a pool of liquid that had spread over his Franklin research. Luckily, Mr. Lewis's books were dry—but Jake's note cards were floating in the puddle!

"My notes!" Jake yelped. He dashed across the room and started frantically mopping up the mess with his baseball jersey. The jersey wasn't very absorbent, though; it splashed the water around as ink stains spread across the slippery fabric.

"Coach is gonna kill me!" Jake said through gritted teeth. Then he spun around to confront

Julia. "You know you're not supposed to be in here!"

Julia wasn't intimidated. She pulled herself up to her full height and yelled back, "You didn't tell me about Ms. Fitzgerald! That wasn't very nice!"

"You didn't need to know!" Jake shot back. "I can't believe this is happening again. Ms. Fitzgerald is here to help *me* with *my* project, and you've just barged in and distracted her . . . just like you distracted Sir Isaac . . . I bet you tripped in those dumb heels and spilled my water all over my notes!"

"I did *not!*" Julia said indignantly.

Ms. Fitzgerald stepped forward, her hands up. "That was my fault, and I'm sorry," she said. "I should've checked the room for glass. Sometimes those high Cs sneak up on me."

"Wait a minute," Jake said. "You broke a glass with your *voice*?"

"It happens," Ms. Fitzgerald said sheepishly.

"And Ms. Fitzgerald's going to teach me how to do it!" Julia said gleefully.

Jake shook his head. "That's *exactly* what I was saying," he said. "When I left, Ms. Fitzgerald was working on my history project. But when I came back, she's giving you singing lessons! My presentation's not finished, I don't have a costume, I don't have any props, I don't have any intros. At this rate, not only am I going to fail, I'm going to be the worst Franklin in the history of Franklin Elementary School!"

"No, you won't," Ms. Fitzgerald spoke up. "Jake, I've got just the thing for your gig."

"Really?" Jake asked. If there was any progress on his project—even just a little bit—maybe he wouldn't be doomed to failure after all.

Just then, Mom's voice floated up the stairs. "Jake! Someone's at the door for you!"

CHAPTER 6

"You two—don't do *anything*," Jake said. "I'll be right back."

Jake ran to the stairs, then slid down the banister to the first floor. Mom was standing in the front hall, barely managing to hide her smile.

"What's going on?" Jake asked.

"See for yourself," she said, stifling a laugh before returning to her office.

Jake opened the front door—and nearly burst out laughing himself. Emerson was standing on the doorstep, wearing a funny-looking wig that was part bald head, part flowing gray hair. A pair of old-fashioned half-moon spectacles was perched on the tip of his nose.

"Emerson?" Jake asked incredulously.

"I went to work with my mom today," he replied. "And she said that we could raid the costume department for our presentations. I think you'll be all set . . . if you want to be . . . I mean, the wig and glasses were from the Ebenezer Scrooge costume, but I don't think anybody will know."

"They're perfect," Jake said. "Thanks. I didn't know what I was going to do for my costume! Do you, uh, want to come in?"

"Sure," Emerson said.

The boys stood in an awkward silence for a moment. Jake had a feeling that Emerson didn't know what to say, either. Then they spoke at the exact same time.

"So, I'm—"

"I'm really—"

"Me, too," Jake said. Then he and Emerson exchanged a grin. They didn't need to say anything else.

Emerson followed Jake upstairs. "How's it going with Ms. Fitzgerald?" he asked. "Do you think she's mad at me about the other day?"

"Nah," Jake replied. "I don't think she understood why you were so upset, though. I mean, everybody else she's ever met is excited to get her autograph. Has your dad noticed yet?"

Emerson shook his head. "But it's only a matter of time," he said fretfully. "Every day I wonder—is it today? Sometimes I wish he knew just so I wouldn't have it hanging over my head."

"It was so tiny," Jake said. "Maybe he'll never notice."

"Maybe," Emerson replied. But he didn't sound convinced.

When they walked into Jake's room, Julia took

one look at Emerson and burst out laughing. "You look silly!" she said.

"Hey, don't be rude," Jake told her. "Emerson's helping me with my project."

But Emerson was already pulling off the wig. "I don't even know why I'm still wearing this thing," he said. "It's kind of itchy."

"Great," Jake said. He held the rubbery bald part between his thumb and forefinger like it was an old banana peel. Then he turned to Ms. Fitzgerald.

"You were just about to tell me your big idea," he reminded her.

Ms. Fitzgerald's eyes lit up. "Oh yes!" she replied. "I wrote a little song—"

"A song?" Jake interrupted her. "Ms. Fitzgerald—I can't sing."

"Nonsense! Everyone can sing," she said. "Show me what you've got, Jake, and when you're done, I'll give you a few pointers."

She held out a tiny scrap of paper. Jake was

about to take it when Ms. Fitzgerald spoke again.

"Best put on your costume first," she told him. "That'll really help you get in the groove."

Jake slipped on the glasses and draped the wig over his head. Emerson was right. It was itchy.

"You look like you're feeling it already!" Ms. Fitzgerald said as she handed over the lyrics. "It goes a little something like this . . . *Doot-n-doot-n-du-du-dow-dow!* Hit it, Jake!"

Jake took a deep breath and started to sing.

> *"Benjamin Franklin!*
> *We all oughta thank him!*
> *He could turn a phrase*
> *Print papers for days*
> *Kite-flying, catch-lightning,*
> *Constitution-signing*
> *Founding Father*
> *Mmmm, yeah!"*

Somewhere downstairs, Flapjack howled unhappily. There were two more verses, but a funny snorting sound in the room interrupted Jake. He glanced up to see Emerson with his hands over his mouth, shaking with silent laughter. Julia's face was bright red from trying to hold it in. Ms. Fitzgerald was the only one who wasn't laughing as she snapped her fingers to the beat.

"Swing it, Jake!" she cheered.

"I, uh, I don't think this is going to work," Jake said. "I really appreciate it, Ms. Fitzgerald. You're a great songwriter. But my presentation's supposed to be first person . . . you know, something like 'I'm Benjamin Franklin and I was born in seventeen-oh-six.'"

"Well, that's not a problem," Ms. Fitzgerald replied. "I'll just make a few adjustments."

Jake grimaced. There was no way he would sing this song in front of the entire school. *No way.*

Then Emerson tried to help. "Ms. Fitzgerald," he began, "your song is great. It's just that

Jake . . . well . . . you and I both know he doesn't have the chops."

Jake didn't know what Emerson was talking about, but he had a feeling he was being insulted. "What does that even mean?" he demanded.

Emerson turned around and gave Jake a look. "Play along," he muttered under his breath.

Ms. Fitzgerald, however, wasn't convinced. "Jake has raw natural talent," she declared. "Trust me, boys, I speak from experience. A song-and-dance routine is the way to get the audience on their feet."

"Yeah—they'll be running for the doors," Julia joked.

Emerson snort-laughed again.

"Ha ha, ha ha," Jake said sarcastically. "Glad everybody's so *entertained*."

"What did I tell you!" Ms. Fitzgerald crowed triumphantly. "It's working already."

Jake shook his head and walked over to his desk. His note cards were still soaked, but maybe once they dried he could try reading them aloud. Maybe he could cobble them into something that sounded like a speech. It would be better than nothing. It would be a *lot* better than a disastrous song-and-dance routine.

Emerson followed him over to the desk. "Jake, you've gotta try the song again," he urged. "Ms. Fitzgerald is a total pro. If she says it will work—"

"It won't work," Jake interrupted him. "Come on, dude. You were snort-laughing."

"I don't snort when I laugh!" Emerson argued, looking embarrassed. "And I only laughed because I wasn't expecting you to, uh, sing."

"Yeah, well, nobody else will be 'expecting' it, either," Jake said. "I wish I could sing and dance. I wish it could be that easy. But it's not. And I wish that somebody else—*anybody else*—could help me—"

POP!

CHAPTER 7

"Fire!" Emerson yelled as he leaped back from the desk. He grabbed Julia and threw her to the ground. "Stop! Drop! Roll!"

"Emerson! Chill!" Jake said, coughing on the familiar cloud of smoke. "It's not—"

"Get down and belly-crawl to the door!" Emerson hollered from the ground.

Jake reached down, grabbed the neck of Emerson's T-shirt, and dragged him to his feet.

"It's not a fire," he repeated. "It's magic. It's the Wishing Well."

Emerson's eyes bugged out. "You mean there's a tiny genius right *here*? Who just appeared out of nowhere?"

"I think so," Jake replied. "That's how it's always happened before." He hadn't meant to wish for another helper—the words had just kind of slipped out—but Jake had to admit he couldn't wait to discover who it would be.

A miniature man stood on Jake's desk, wearing a plum-colored silk suit with a long coat, short pants, and matching vest. His ruffled white shirt matched his stockings, and the shiny buckles on his shoes reflected the sparks that were still twinkling. The bald head, the wavy gray hair, the spectacles . . . it was all starting to add up.

"Drat this blasted fog!" he grumbled, peering through his glasses. "Give me a lightning storm any day. With all its ferocity, at least it's soon to clear."

That's when Jake realized that the man was carrying a kite . . . and a tiny brass key! Now there was no doubt in his mind that the Wishing Well had finally sent Benjamin Franklin to help with his project!

Jake's triumphant fist pump sliced through the smoke. "Yes!" he cheered. With Benjamin Franklin's help on his Benjamin Franklin project, Jake would get an A for sure!

"Is that . . . ?" Emerson whispered.

Jake nodded. "I think so," he replied. "Excuse me . . . sir?"

The man turned around. When he saw Jake, he gasped and stumbled backwards. His shoe slipped on a pencil, causing the man to fall into the puddle Jake still hadn't cleaned up. But the man was so horrified that he didn't even seem to notice.

"My own self!" the man gasped. "Made large and terrible before my very eyes!"

Too late, Jake remembered that he was still wearing the Benjamin Franklin wig and glasses.

He whipped them off and hid them behind his back. "No!" he said. "My name is Jake and I am *definitely* not you."

Jake held his breath, worried that Mr. Franklin would think Jake was mocking him. Instead, the portly older man started to chuckle. "So it was just a jest. Very good, my lad, very good," he said as he hoisted himself to his feet. Then he crossed his arm over his waist and bowed with a flourish. "Benjamin Franklin, at your service."

"It's incredible to meet you," Jake replied.

Mr. Franklin leaned forward and spoke in a confidential tone. "Was there a passing thunder-shower?" he asked. "It's just that my breeches *are* rather damp."

"Uh . . . no," Jake replied. "It hasn't rained for a couple weeks. Besides, we're indoors."

"Oh yes, I see that now. The fog must've addled my brain," Mr. Franklin said. "How *are* the skies, young sir? My boy, Billy, and I have been waiting for a proper thunderstorm for weeks. You see, my kite is not an ordinary kite, not in the least; I have specially designed it so that it will attract a bolt of lightning. A *conduit*, if you will."

Right, Jake thought, remembering how Mr. Franklin had made a world-changing discovery about electricity by conducting an incredibly dangerous, incredibly daring experiment. He'd flown a kite in the middle of a thunderstorm to prove his theory that bolts of lightning were actually electricity. Leaning down for a closer look, Jake was able to see that the kite had a piece of wire sticking out of the top and a shiny metal key tied to the string.

"You've invented lots of things, haven't you?" Jake asked, the words coming slowly since his brain was busy hatching an idea. Not just any idea, though. This idea was big. It might even be great.

Mr. Franklin's smile looked like the one in the portrait at school: tinged with pride and modesty at the same time. "Well, I daresay I've invented my fair share of items to improve the conditions under which my fellow man toils," he said. "The Glass Armonica, the Long Arm, the Bifocals, the Franklin Stove . . ."

Mr. Franklin was still talking, but Jake was no longer listening. Like a firework, his idea had exploded from one bright spot into dozens of glittering sparks. Maybe Jake's Franklin presentation could focus on all the things he had created or invented! Maybe each introduction could connect one of Franklin's inventions to one of the other historical figures!

Maybe Jake was going to succeed after all!

"Mr. Franklin, I need your help," Jake said urgently. "Can you write down all your inventions for me? Not just the names, but descriptions . . . and maybe little drawings . . ."

"A catalog of my life's work?" Mr. Franklin asked.

"Yes, exactly," Jake said.

Mr. Franklin's brow furrowed. "I should like to help you very much, young man," he replied. "Why, as I wrote in my autobiography, 'As we benefit from the inventions of others, we should be glad to share our own . . . freely and gladly.' Alas, I am at the mercy of the weather. If a storm should arise . . ."

Jake crossed the room and threw back the curtains. "The sun's shining. There aren't any clouds in the sky," he said. "I don't think it's going to rain . . . and it definitely won't be a thunderstorm."

"In that case, I would be most happy to help," Mr. Franklin told Jake. "I appreciate your conscientiousness. As I've always believed, 'By failing to prepare, you are preparing to fail.'"

Jake hurried over to Emerson and explained his plan. "After Mr. Franklin writes down all the awesome things he created, I can turn them into my presentation!" he said excitedly.

"Cool," Emerson replied. "Since your report is under control, do you want to check out the costumes at Mom's work? The costume manager isn't working today, so Mom said we could pick out anything we want to borrow for our presentations."

"Yeah, I guess we should," Jake replied. "But . . . I kind of don't want to interrupt Mr. Franklin. He's just getting started on that list."

"You could leave him here," Emerson suggested. "He's just writing down a list, right? How much trouble could he get into?"

"You don't want to know," Jake replied. But he had a bad feeling that a field trip to the theater would distract Mr. Franklin from helping with his project.

Jake leaned over to Julia. "Will you do me a big favor?" he whispered. "Would you stay here and make sure Mr. Franklin doesn't get into any trouble?"

"Like a *babysitter*?" Julia squealed.

"Yes! Just like a babysitter," Jake told her. He turned to Emerson. "Should we leave Ms. Fitzgerald here, too?"

"Actually, maybe she should come with us," Emerson said. "Maybe if you hang out with Ella Fitzgerald near a stage, you'll understand why the Wishing Well sent her."

"It's worth a try," Jake said. He hurried over to the dollhouse, where Ms. Fitzgerald was practicing her warm-ups again. "Ms. Fitzgerald? Would you like to go to the theater?" he asked. "You could, uh, rehearse on the stage if you'd like?"

"A dress rehearsal?" Ms. Fitzgerald asked brightly. "Why, that sounds like the cat's pajamas!"

CHAPTER 8

The theater where Emerson's mom worked was a short bike ride from Jake's house. Emerson led Jake around back to a plain black door with an intercom next to it. Emerson pressed the buzzer and said, "Hey, Mom! I'm here! With Jake!"

Bzzzzz!

"This is the stage door," Emerson explained. "It's for the actors and crew."

Jake had never been backstage before. The walls were cluttered with posters from past shows, and a few different offices jutted off from the narrow, twisting hallway.

Mrs. Lewis briefly looked up from her computer to wave. "Good luck shopping, boys," she joked.

Jake grimaced. He *hated* shopping. The sooner they found his Ben Franklin costume, the better.

"Where is everybody?" Jake asked Emerson as they went down to the basement.

"Mom says the theater is for night owls," Jake said. "That's when the actors show up for rehearsal and the crew builds the set, and it can get really loud and fun and crazy. The quiet behind-the-scenes work happens during the day. Come on, the costume shop is in here."

Jake followed Emerson into a cavernous room filled with sewing machines, tall mirrors, tables, dressmaker forms, and bolts of fabric in every color and pattern imaginable. The walls were lined with racks of costumes, shelves of hats and wigs, and boxes of shoes.

Jake helped Ms. Fitzgerald climb out of his backpack. She looked around, confused. "Where's the stage?"

"We'll go there next," Jake said.

Emerson yanked some pins out of a tufted pincushion. "Would you like to have a seat?" he asked Ms. Fitzgerald.

She perched on the edge of the pincushion, but even Jake could tell how eager she was to get to the stage. "This will just take a couple minutes," he promised. Then he turned to Emerson. "Where do we begin?"

Emerson glanced at a list on the wall. "What time period would Benjamin Franklin be?" he asked.

"Um . . . colonial, I guess?" Jake said.

"Row C, rack 12," Emerson replied.

Jake and Emerson sifted through all sorts of

old-fashioned clothes—from vests and breeches to tricornered hats and floppy bow ties. Jake pulled on a brown velvet vest. The matching pants looked like they would end just above his knees, with small bows on each side. There was a ruffled, lacy tie attached to an even more ruffled shirt. Jake even found a pair of shoes with stacked heels and shiny buckles. It all *looked* right, but after Jake tried everything on, he had a strange sinking feeling.

"I don't know about this," Jake began.

"What's the matter?" Emerson asked.

"I—don't get me wrong, these costumes are incredible," Jake began. "But . . . isn't everybody going to laugh at me?"

Emerson shrugged. "You have to wear a Benjamin Franklin costume," he pointed out. "This is what they wore back then, I think."

Jake sighed. "Yeah. You're right. And you're lucky. I wish *I* could just wear a baseball uniform."

"Old-fashioned baseball uniforms were dumb-looking, too," Emerson pointed out. "I have to wear my mom's knee socks . . . and tuck in my pants so that the top part is all poofy and baggy!"

"So you're saying I look dumb?" Jake said, smiling so Emerson would know he was joking. He felt a little better, at least, knowing that he wouldn't be the only one all dressed up.

"What do you think, Ms. Fitzgerald?" Jake asked, peering into the mirror.

But there was no response. And that was when Jake realized that Ms. Fitzgerald had been silent for several minutes now. That wasn't like her. He spun around . . . and realized that the pincushion was empty.

"Emerson—she's gone!" Jake exclaimed.

"What do you mean—*gone*?" Emerson yelped.

"What do you think I mean?" Jake said. "Ms. Fitzgerald is gone—disappeared—vanished! Come on! We have to find her!"

Jake and Emerson scoured the entire costume

shop, peeking behind sewing machines and searching stacks of fabric. There was no sign of Ms. Fitzgerald anywhere. She had disappeared without a trace.

"She's not here," Jake finally said.

"We have to find her before anyone else does!" Emerson exclaimed. "If my mom . . . or the crew . . . oh, man, the actors have rehearsal soon!"

"Stay calm," Jake told him. "Let's think it through. If *you* were Ella Fitzgerald, and you found yourself in a theater, where would you go?"

Jake had barely asked the question before the answer occurred to him and Emerson at the same time.

"The stage!" they yelled.

The boys clambered up the stairs as fast as they could, their footsteps clattering through the nearly empty theater. As they went backstage, Jake strained his ears. Was that . . . *singing*?

Emerson pulled the curtain back a few inches. The boys peeked out at the pitch-black house, where a single spotlight sliced through the darkness, illuminating a perfect circle in the center of the stage.

In the middle of it stood itty-bitty Ella Fitzgerald.

Even though she was only three inches tall, Jake recognized the pure star power that radiated from her. Jake stood perfectly still, not fidgeting, not whispering. Just listening. Just marveling that anybody in the whole wide world could have a voice like that.

When Ms. Fitzgerald's song ended, the very last note hung in the air, quivering. Jake started applauding wildly. It was the only thing to do.

At the sound, Ms. Fitzgerald glanced over to the wings. "Hello, boys," she called, waving. "I thought I might as well start rehearsing. Great space, isn't it?"

"Ms. Fitzgerald," Jake said, "that was—you were—*wow*."

"Incredible," added Emerson.

"The stage!" Jake continued. "It was like you *owned* it!"

There was a mysterious quality to Ms. Fitzgerald's smile, as if she knew a secret. "Well, right then, I felt as if I did," she said. "That's called stage presence. And you don't need to be a singer to have it."

"Can you teach me?" Jake asked. With Mr. Franklin's first-person advice and a fraction of Ms. Fitzgerald's performing skills, the Living History project suddenly seemed a lot more manageable.

"It would be my honor," Ms. Fitzgerald replied.

CHAPTER 9

Just like that, the rest of Jake's Living History project fell into place. He used his now-dry note cards and Mr. Franklin's inventions to connect Benjamin Franklin's life to the other historical figures in the show. He practiced his speech every night before bed. He didn't even mind the itchy wig for his costume. It was a lot better than the thunky, clunky, thick-heeled shoes he had to wear. Best of all, Ms. Turner had reviewed everyone's note cards . . . and given Jake's a big red check-plus. It was the first check-plus he'd ever received.

On Thursday morning, Jake woke up even before his alarm clock. He stared at the ceiling in the gray light of early morning, wondering what had awakened him. Then Jake heard it—a long, low rumble in the distance.

Thunder.

Jake sat up in bed. He wasn't scared of electrical storms—that was Julia's fear—but he had a heavy feeling of foreboding. Like something was coming. Something . . . bad.

And that's when Jake remembered: Living History Night was in a few short hours. Soon it would be over. Soon it would be just a memory. Soon Jake would never have to wear that silly-looking Benjamin Franklin costume again.

But right then, at that moment, it loomed large and terrifying. There was another rumble of thunder, and Jake ducked his head under his pillow. If only he could sleep through the next twelve hours and wake up when it was all over.

"Arise and shine, young lad!" Mr. Franklin called out gleefully. Ms. Fitzgerald's voice, singing up and down the scales, drifted from the dollhouse. Jake sighed. There was no way he could go back to sleep now. And, as he glanced out the window, he saw the sun peeking out from behind the clouds.

Hopefully, that was a good sign!

At school, all the other students seemed louder and more excited than usual—except for Jake. He got quieter and quieter as the day went on. Then Jake noticed that Emerson seemed pretty unhappy, too. "You okay?" Jake said. "You look kind of worried."

"You bet I'm worried," Emerson said. "My dad is teaching his classes about Ella Fitzgerald's music today. I left the house before he packed up his albums, but there's no way he hasn't seen her autograph by now. No way. My life is basically over after Living History Night."

"Maybe not," Jake said. "Maybe you'll just get grounded for a couple days."

Before the final bell, Ms. Turner had an important announcement. "Remember, we'll be meeting in the classroom at six o'clock tonight," she said. "Wear your costumes! And don't be nervous. I know you're all going to do a great job."

The quivery feeling in Jake's stomach was getting worse. At least he had baseball practice to distract him from his nervousness.

But by the time Jake and Emerson arrived at Franklin Field, the sun had disappeared behind a thick wall of dark clouds. Coach Carlson was waiting by the gate. "Sorry, guys," he said. "We're in the middle of a severe thunderstorm warning. Practice is canceled."

"Okay," Jake said, trying to hide his disappointment. It wasn't even raining yet, so the forecast must've been really bad.

Suddenly, Jake gasped.

Severe thunderstorm warning.

This was the opportunity Mr. Franklin had been waiting for—and Jake had left him all alone!

Coach Carlson and Emerson both gave Jake funny looks. "Everything okay?" asked Coach.

"My—window," Jake replied, thinking fast. "I left it open! Gotta go—close it—before the rain!"

Then he took off running, all the way home.

Sure enough, Mr. Franklin was standing on the windowsill, puttering with the wire on the top of his kite. "*Halloooo*, young squire!" he called when he saw Jake. "We've been blessed with a hearty gale, and if those clouds are any indication, we shall soon be the recipients of a most wild and fearsome squall!"

Jake somehow managed not to groan. "Mr. Franklin," he began, "I know I told you that you could . . . do your experiment if we got a thunderstorm. But the truth is, it's extremely dangerous. Besides, we already know that lightning is electricity."

"Ah, ah, ah!" Mr. Franklin replied, waggling his finger. "We don't *know* it, we *suspect* it, and therein lies a world of difference! Besides, as I wrote in *The Way to Wealth*, 'Never leave that till tomorrow, which you can do today'!"

"Be-bop-ba-ba-deet-deet-deet-daa!"

Ms. Fitzgerald was scatting again. There was too much going on—Jake shook his head, as if that could help him focus—

Knock, knock, knock!

"No!" Jake yelled.

"Excuse me?" Mom's voice carried through the closed door.

"Um—I'm changing into my costume," he called back. "Just a minute!"

"Oh, good, I was checking to make sure you're getting ready," she replied. "Come down when you're done; I made some sandwiches to tide you over. Dad wants to go out to dinner after the show. We can invite Emerson's family, too."

Mom said it so lightly—"after the show"—like it was no big deal, but Jake wasn't sure he'd survive that long. Just during the last minute, Mr. Franklin had nudged the window open wider.

"Stop!" Jake yelped as he ran back across the room. He had to convince Mr. Franklin that this was a terrible idea. If Mr. Franklin attracted a bolt of lightning with his special kite, the whole house could burn down!

"There's, uh, too many trees in the backyard," Jake said, thinking fast. "Your kite could get tangled. Plus, lightning could strike the trees—instead of your kite."

Discouragement passed over Mr. Franklin's face like a fast-moving cloud.

"But if you come with me to Living History Night, there's a big field behind the school," Jake babbled. "Plenty of space to fly a kite and catch a lightning bolt . . ."

Jake crossed his fingers, hoping Mr. Franklin

would agree. With any luck, the storm would blow over by the time they got to Franklin Elementary for Living History Night.

Mr. Franklin thought about it for a moment. Then he nodded his head. "Very well," he replied. "I've waited this long. There's no harm in waiting a bit longer."

Then he turned to Ms. Fitzgerald. "My dear lady, may I impose upon you to watch the heavens for me from here?" he asked. "I shall make a kite of your very own, and should the conditions look favorable—"

"Nope. No way. Absolutely not," Jake interrupted. "You can't ask Ms. Fitzgerald to do something so dangerous."

"I wouldn't mind helping," Ms. Fitzgerald spoke up.

Jake looked at her, aghast.

"But I'm coming to Living History Night, too," she continued.

"You're—what?" Jake asked.

"Why, I wouldn't miss it for the world!" Ms. Fitzgerald declared. "I'm sure there will be a full house. I have a feeling it's going to be a *very* well attended event."

Jake narrowed his eyes. Was Ms. Fitzgerald thinking that *she* might perform, too?

"Jake! Sandwiches!" Mom called from downstairs.

Jake had to make a decision—fast. "Okay," he said. "You can both come. But for the *last* time, you've *got* to stay out of sight!"

The tiny geniuses didn't hear him—or maybe they just pretended that they didn't hear him. Mr. Franklin was already packing his kite as Ms. Fitzgerald's voice filled the room once more, dancing up and down the scale.

Jake could only hope he hadn't made a big mistake.

CHAPTER 10

Going to school at the end of the day always felt wrong to Jake. The sky was darkening rapidly—not just from the setting sun but the gathering clouds as well. All the classrooms blazed with light, making Franklin Elementary School's windows glow.

As Dad parked the car, Jake watched other families hurrying toward the school. He saw a couple other fourth graders in their costumes—including Jonah, who was dressed up as William Shakespeare with a big, ruffly collar around his neck. That made Jake feel a little less self-conscious about his Benjamin Franklin costume.

Before they walked into school, Mom gave Jake a fast hug. "Proud of you," she whispered near his ear. "You're going to be terrific!"

Jake wished he could be so certain. But even his smile felt wobbly.

"Go get 'em, champ!" Dad said, clapping Jake on the shoulder. "Remember, if all else fails, make 'em laugh. You're a very funny guy, you know."

"We'll be sitting front and center," Mom promised. "We don't want to miss a thing!"

Are you sure about that? Jake wished he could ask. But all he said was, "See you after the show."

"Break a leg!"

Dad's voice echoed down the hall, following Jake as he went to his classroom. It was pandemonium! All the other students were goofing off like it was the last day of school, laughing loudly and messing around. Sebastian, wearing a wetsuit for his Jacques Cousteau costume, was pelting the other kids with rubber fish.

It's easy for everybody else, Jake realized. *They just have to stand up there and talk for a minute or two. Not the whole time, practically.* Even if they were nervous, they knew their parts were small— and would be over soon.

Jake glanced around. No one was paying attention to him, so he slipped into a corner, unzipped his backpack, and peeked inside. "You two okay in there?" he whispered.

"Well . . ." Ms. Fitzgerald spoke up. "The air *is* rather close."

"An understatement!" Mr. Franklin huffed as he hoisted himself up. "Your knapsack smells like a rancid cheese board."

Then Mr. Franklin spotted his portrait on the wall. "Who is that handsome devil?" he asked.

"Why, he looks so familiar, I almost wonder if he is a distant relation!"

"Yeah . . . you could say that," Jake replied. But before he could tell Mr. Franklin that Franklin Elementary School was actually named after him, Jake heard a familiar laugh behind him. It wasn't a friendly laugh, either.

Aiden, Jake thought in dismay.

"Wow, I didn't know that Ben Franklin was the kind of nutcase who stood around talking to himself," Aiden announced loudly. His fancy Napoleon costume, with all its medals and swoops of gold braid, seemed to make him even more unpleasant.

Jake clamped his backpack closed before Mr. Franklin had a chance to protest and make things a thousand times worse.

"I wasn't talking to myself," he told Aiden. "I was . . . practicing."

Aiden laughed again, right in Jake's face. "You? Practicing? Yeah, right!" he said. "Don't worry,

Everfail. Nobody will be surprised when you bomb. It's not like you'll be letting anyone down. We're all expecting it."

Jake's face was on fire. He *really* wanted to tell Aiden exactly what he thought of him . . . It would feel *so* good . . .

Just then, Ms. Turner hurried into the room. Her arms were full of programs for the event.

"Oh, good, Jake and Aiden—just who I was looking for!" she said brightly. "Aiden, you look ready. Would you stand at the entrance of the auditorium to hand out these programs to our guests?"

Jake could tell Aiden was trying to smile, but all he could manage was a smirk. "Of course, Ms. Turner," he said.

Jake was so relieved to see Aiden leave that he didn't notice the flicker of light in the darkening sky.

"Now, Jake," Ms. Turner said, turning her full attention to him. "I'd like to have a word with you in the hall."

Jake grabbed his backpack, but Ms. Turner shook her head. "Just leave your props—this will only take a minute," she said.

Leave my backpack? Jake thought in a panic. Slowly, he lowered it to the floor. A bad feeling washed over him.

Emerson! Jake thought suddenly. Emerson would understand that Jake's backpack could not, under any circumstances, be left unattended.

Jake tried to catch Emerson's eye. But he was too busy practicing his Jackie Robinson batting poses. He never looked at Jake—not even once. Jake had no choice but to leave his backpack behind and hope that Ms. Turner's talk would be fast.

The hallway was surprisingly quiet compared to the chaos of the classroom.

"How are you feeling, Jake?" Ms. Turner asked.

Ms. Turner's smile was so kind. For the first time, Jake let himself say the word aloud. "Nervous," he admitted. "*Really* nervous."

"Well, I'd be nervous if you weren't nervous," Ms. Turner told him.

Jake's face scrunched up in confusion. Had he heard her right?

"The fact that you're nervous tells me that you've taken this assignment seriously," she continued. "I thought your note cards looked great. I love the creative angle for your introductions!"

"Really?" Jake asked.

"Really," Ms. Turner said. "You're going to be an incredible Benjamin Franklin. Everybody's rooting for you!"

Aiden's mocking face flashed before Jake's eyes for a split second and he thought, *Not everybody*.

Then something surprising happened. Jake thought of Emerson and Hannah. Elizabeth and Marco. Clara and Sam. Principal Barron and Coach Carlton. And Mom and Dad and Julia and even, Jake realized, Ms. Fitzgerald and Mr. Franklin. They were all rooting for him—just like Ms. Turner said.

And Jake realized that maybe Aiden didn't matter so much after all. When he smiled at Ms. Turner, his smile wasn't wobbly anymore.

Ms. Turner glanced at her watch. "Fifteen minutes to go. Is there anything I can do for you before the show starts?"

"I don't think so," Jake replied. For the first time, he felt ready. Almost ready, anyway.

Jake followed Ms. Turner back into the classroom. It was still a jumble of activity. Jake could hear his classmates practicing their speeches all at once.

"All right, everyone," Ms. Turner said loudly over all the commotion. "You should be on your last practice. Now is a good time to go to the bathroom. We're going backstage in ten minutes!"

Suddenly, Jake's eyes focused like a laser on the window. It was open, just a crack.

But the classroom windows were never open.

Especially not at night.

There was a rumble of thunder, loud enough for Jake to hear it clearly over all the noise in the classroom.

Oh no, Jake thought.

He had a very bad feeling that Mr. Franklin was about to make history—all over again!

Jake forced himself to cross the room slowly, instead of racing to the window in a panic. He didn't want to attract any attention—especially since he didn't know how difficult it would be to coax Mr. Franklin inside.

Jake leaned against the wall and glanced outside. It was almost too dark to see, but Jake could just make out Mr. Franklin's and Ms. Fitzgerald's silhouettes against the sky—and Mr. Franklin's tiny kite, bobbing in the breeze!

A bolt of lightning flashed in the distance. The key on the kite string glinted.

Jake inched the window open a little more and whispered, "Mr. Franklin! You *have* to come in! This is incredibly dangerous!"

"That's what I've been trying to tell him!" Ms. Fitzgerald said.

Flash!

Crack!

Boom!

That bolt of lightning—and rumble of thunder—was even closer.

"Not much longer now!" Mr. Franklin said gleefully. "Thor is wielding his mighty hammer tonight!"

"What are you talking about?" Jake said. "Get inside!"

"Not until—"

Mr. Franklin didn't finish his sentence. He didn't need to. At that moment, the flash of lightning blazed so brightly that Jake was momentarily blinded. Thunder boomed, rattling the windows. The lightning hit the kite, transforming it into a tiny blazing fireball in the night sky. Then the crackling bolt zipped down the kite string.

The key blazed—

Mr. Franklin's hair stood on end—

His glasses smoked—

And then something even worse happened. Jake wasn't quite sure what—

Or how—

But the lightning was unstoppable in its search for metal—a *conduit*, Jake remembered somehow—

Boom!

The explosion—and it was definitely an explosion—scattered sparks high into the air.

Then the entire school was plunged into darkness!

CHAPTER 11

"AHHHHHHHHHHHHHHHHHHHHHHHHHHHHHHHH!"

The screams weren't just coming from Ms. Turner's class; they were coming from every kid in school, and they echoed down the halls and through the classrooms.

"It's just a power failure! No need to panic," Ms. Turner was saying, but no one was listening.

Flash!

Crack!

Boom!

Another bolt of lightning lit up the sky. It illuminated Mr. Franklin and Ms. Fitzgerald, who were miraculously still on the ledge. Jake lunged forward, thrust his hand through the window, and grabbed them both.

"Are you okay?" he asked frantically. "Can you hear me? Say something! Anything!"

Flash!

In the brief glow of lightning, Jake saw Mr. Franklin, singed and soaked, grin up at him. "Anything!" he quipped.

Ms. Fitzgerald couldn't quite stifle her laugh. But Jake didn't think it was funny.

Crack!

"I hope you're happy," he snapped. "My school got hit by lightning, and now the power's out, and—"

Jake stopped talking abruptly. What would happen if the lights didn't come back on? Would Living History Night be canceled?

BOOM!

"Ahhhhhhhhhhhhhhhhhhhhhhhhhhhhh!" everyone screamed again.

"Children. It's just a thunderstorm," Ms. Turner said. "Please stay calm."

In the dark, Jake could hear a rustling noise. Then Ms. Turner held up her cell phone like a flashlight. It provided just enough light for Jake to see everyone in the room.

There was a *bzzz—bzzzzzzzz—*

Then, in a sudden *whoosh*, the lights blazed on. Jake blinked in the sudden brightness, then shoved Mr. Franklin and Ms. Fitzgerald in his backpack before anyone could see them.

"Oh, good," Ms. Turner said. "The emergency generator kicked in—and not a moment too soon. Class, please line up at the door. It's almost time for Living History Night to begin!"

But—the last practice, Jake thought frantically. He glanced around, but everyone else was already moving toward the door. He'd missed his chance for one final run-through.

"Make room for Benjamin Franklin at the front of the line!" Ms. Turner announced.

A sick, swooping feeling came over Jake as his classmates cleared a path for him. It was a cross between riding a roller coaster and missing a step on the stairs. Jake tried to squash it down as he moved to the front of the line, the heels of his Franklin shoes clattering on the linoleum.

"Lead the way, Ben Franklin," Ms. Turner's voice rang out.

It was all happening so fast—*too fast*, Jake thought, but there was no way to slow it down. The other fourth-grade classes were filing into the hall, too. Whenever someone saw Jake in his Franklin costume, though, they moved out of the way. The last thing Jake wanted to do was lead—but he had no choice.

When the fourth graders reached the auditorium, they crowded backstage. Nobody was messing around now. Even though the curtains were closed, Jake could hear the muffled voices of the people who'd filled the auditorium—his family, and Emerson's family, and all his other friends' families . . .

Jake closed his eyes as another wave of nervousness washed over him.

Then he felt someone tap his shoulder. It was Ms. Turner.

"Ready?" she mouthed.

No! Jake wanted to yell. But he knew that wasn't an option. So he nodded and followed Ms. Turner to the side of the stage, where he tucked his backpack in the corner. The lights over the audience went out—on purpose this time. A bright spotlight lit up the stage.

It was time.

Jake took a deep breath and began to walk onstage.

Jake would never know exactly how it happened, but his shoes—those stupid shoes, with their dumb buckles and ridiculous heels—somehow snagged the stockings on his right leg. He hopped, trying to loosen it—knowing as the audience giggled that he must look so foolish—

And then something even worse happened.

Ka-thunk-thump-THUD.

Jake went flying in a spectacularly disastrous, skid-across-the-stage, land-flat-on-his-face fall. He actually heard the audience gasp as his spectacles flew one way and his wig flew the other. Jake would've gasped, too, but his fall had knocked the wind out of him.

A terrible silence followed. Then Jake heard it. Laughter.

People were *laughing* at him.

Jake grabbed the wig, scrambled to his feet, and rushed offstage. He huddled in a dark corner, behind the curtain, where he was sure that no one would find him. He rubbed his side. His ribs were really sore, and his elbow *killed*, but that's not why hot tears filled his eyes.

I will not cry, Jake thought fiercely. *I will* not *cry*.

Suddenly, Jake felt someone tug on his Franklin coat.

"Jake! What are you doing?" Ms. Fitzgerald asked urgently. "You've got to get back out there! The audience is waiting."

"Can't," Jake said through gritted teeth.

Ms. Fitzgerald pulled herself up to her full height—all three inches. "And why not?" she demanded. "Because of a little stumble?"

"Little stumble?" Jake repeated. "It was a total wipeout! I blew it—without even saying a word, I ruined Living History Night!"

"The only way you'll ruin Living History Night is if you leave it without a host," Mr. Franklin spoke up, his forehead deeply furrowed. "I have long said, 'Do not fear mistakes. You will know failure. Continue to reach out.'"

"Jake. Listen to me," Ms. Fitzgerald said. Her voice, usually so melodious, was now lower and urgent. It commanded attention.

"I didn't have an easy start," she began. "There was a time when I didn't even have a place to live, or any family to speak of. But I did have a dream, and I figured dancing at Amateur Night at the Apollo Theater was a good way to make it come true. When I got up onstage, my knees knocking and my heart hammering, well, I couldn't dance a lick. So I opened my mouth to sing instead—but only the worst, warbling, chicken-scratch sound came out of my throat! And the audience *booed*. Jake, my moment was almost over before it had even begun."

Jake was holding his breath.

"Then the emcee said, 'Give her another chance, folks.' That was it, Jake—my chance. And so I sang. In a tattered dress and old men's boots and after my bad start, I sang *anyway*. This time, it came out right. And the audience? They begged for more. That was the moment Lady Ella was born.

"So the question I think about sometimes, late

at night," Ms. Fitzgerald continued, "is not, 'What if I didn't go on that stage?' It's, 'What if I didn't *try again*?'"

Jake nodded. "Okay," he whispered. "I understand. Thank you."

He paused for one more moment—one more deep breath—before putting on his wig and spectacles and straightening his coat. Then Jake strode onstage with purposeful strides, remembering what Dad had said: *Make 'em laugh.*

Jake turned to the audience. The spotlight was so bright in his eyes that he couldn't see, which almost made it easier. He remembered Ms. Fitzgerald's stage presence tips from their afternoon at the Wonderland Stage and planted his feet firmly, pushed back his shoulders, and grinned at the audience.

"Who's ready to *fall* into history with the fourth grade of Franklin Elementary School?" Jake said in his loudest, clearest voice.

A beat.

And then—laughter! The good kind! And applause—lots of it!

Jake's smile grew even bigger. The audience was cheering for him not just because he'd made a joke but because he had tried again. A fall wasn't going to keep him down—and they loved it.

They loved *him*.

"Wolfgang Amadeus Mozart was a famous composer—but imagine how much more famous he'd have been if he'd written music for an instrument I invented, the Glass Armonica," Jake said in his best Ben Franklin voice. "No, your ears aren't playing tricks on you. I said *armonica*, not *harmonica*. Who needs the extra 'h' anyway?"

The audience was chuckling as Lila, wearing a wild-looking Mozart wig, walked onto the stage.

When Lila finished, Jake glanced at the side of the stage. He spotted Sebastian wearing his Jacques Cousteau costume—complete with rubber fish—waiting for his cue. "Everyone knows about the famous ocean explorer Jacques Cousteau,"

Jake announced. "But did you know that *I* invented the swim fins? It's true—except I designed them to be worn on the hands, not the feet!"

One by one, Jake's classmates approached the side of the stage, awaiting their introductions. With every line, every joke, Jake felt stronger. More confident. He almost wondered why he had ever dreaded Living History Night.

All too soon, the end of the show arrived. Jake took a deep breath and faced the audience for the last time.

"Some people call me a Founding Father because I signed the Declaration of Independence and helped write the Constitution of the United States of America," Jake announced. "Millions of people around the world wear one of my inventions, the bifocal glasses, every single day. And if you're *really* lucky, you may have even seen me on the hundred-dollar bill."

Jake rubbed his thumb and fingers together, making everyone laugh again.

"But if there was one way I'd want the world to remember me," Jake-as-Franklin said, "it would be for always wanting to make it better. And I know I speak for all of us who've told you about our lives tonight when I say we hope we've made your world a little better, too."

Jake crossed his arm over his waist and bowed with a big flourish, just the way Mr. Franklin had when they'd first met.

The lights dimmed to black.

For half a moment, there was silence.

And then—the roar of applause!

Jake's heart was hammering again, but with excitement this time. He stood up as his classmates joined him onstage and the applause grew even louder. With the stage lights so bright, Jake couldn't be certain, but he thought the audience had started to rise in a standing ovation.

And it was all for the fourth grade of Franklin Elementary School!

CHAPTER 12

Jake's smile felt like it had been stuck on with superglue. As his classmates crowded around, high-fiving him and slapping him on the back, he knew that he hadn't let anyone down.

Ms. Turner and Principal Bannon approached.

"Well done, Jake," Principal Bannon said in his big, booming voice as he shook Jake's hand.

"I knew you'd do a great job!" added Ms. Turner. "I'm sure your family can't wait to see you."

That reminded Jake of someone else who probably wanted to see him, too. He slipped away to
the quiet corner where he'd left his backpack—
and Ms. Fitzgerald and Mr. Franklin.

"Oh, Jake!" Ms. Fitzgerald cried, clapping her
hands together. "You really tore it up out there!"

"I couldn't have done a better job myself of
playing . . . myself," Mr. Franklin announced.

"And I couldn't have done it without the two of
you," Jake said.

A sizzling sound, like lightning tearing through
velvet, filled Jake's ears. He watched in astonishment as a section of the theater curtain burned
away, creating a glittering hole. There was the
sound of a faraway trumpet . . . the *rat-a-tat* of a
drum set . . .

"That's my cue," Ms. Fitzgerald said, her eyes
shining with happiness.

"Allow me, my lady," Mr. Franklin said as he
offered his arm.

Ms. Fitzgerald linked her arm through his, and

together they disappeared through the enchanted rip in the curtain. With another burst of light, the hole sealed behind them. Just like that, there was no sign that Ms. Fitzgerald or Mr. Franklin had ever been there.

But they *had* been. Jake knew it.

"They're . . . gone?" Emerson asked.

Jake spun around. He didn't know that Emerson had come up behind him. "Yeah," he said, a strange sadness creeping into his voice. "The Heroes of History aren't really good at saying good-bye."

"I guess not," replied Emerson.

"Oh!" Jake said. "I almost forgot. My mom invited you guys out to dinner with us."

"I hope my parents say yes—since it might be my last meal." Emerson was trying to be funny, but his forehead was all scrunched up with worry. "When my dad sees what Ms. Fitzgerald did to his album . . ."

"You haven't seen him since this morning?" Jake asked.

Emerson shook his head. "Might as well get it over with," he said.

Together, the two boys walked out of the auditorium. Ms. Turner had been right—Jake's family was standing right by the door, ready to pounce with hugs and high fives.

"That's my boy!" Dad said.

"You were incredible!" Mom told Jake, kissing his cheek right there in front of everybody.

"Did you get a really bad boo-boo when you fell?" Julia asked anxiously.

Emerson's family was standing across the hall, and Mr. Lewis was being really loud. *I hope he's not yelling at Emerson*, Jake worried. He glanced over at them and was surprised to see that Mr. Lewis was beaming.

"How is it possible I didn't notice it before?" Mr. Lewis was saying. "All this time, I've owned an autographed Ella Fitzgerald album! Can you believe it, E?"

"No, Dad," Emerson said, choking a little as he tried not to laugh. "I can't."

"Her signature's really tiny; that's the only explanation I can think of," Mr. Lewis continued, shaking his head in amazement. "My poor students—I couldn't stop talking about it. Lady Ella signed my record! I can't wait to show you!"

Jake met Emerson's eyes, and they shared a knowing smile.

"Jake!" Mrs. Lewis said, crossing the hall. "Bravo! How come you've been hiding your talent all these years? I *expect* you to audition for our next show, young man."

Jake grinned at her. "Maybe I will," he replied, "as long as you don't need me to sing!"

A NOTE FROM THE AUTHOR

Ella Fitzgerald, known as the First Lady of Song, was one of the greatest American singers of all time. She was born in Virginia on April 25, 1917. When she was young, Ella and her mother moved north to Yonkers, New York, where Ella's stepfather and younger half sister joined the family. The family struggled financially, but everyone worked hard to make ends meet—including Ella.

When Ella was fifteen years old, tragedy struck when her mother died, turning Ella's life upside down. Ella moved in with an aunt, skipped school, and was then sent to an overcrowded reform school. When Ella could no longer bear living in such miserable conditions, she ran away and became homeless.

Within two years, though, everything changed when Ella entered to compete in Amateur Night at the Apollo Theater. At first Ella planned to dance, but at the last minute, she decided to sing instead. After a rocky start, Ella was given a second chance at the microphone—and her incredible voice stunned the crowd. Ella was stunned, too. In the spotlight, all her shyness melted away, and she felt completely at home.

A combination of incredible talent, dedication, and hard work brought Ella international fame for her glorious voice. The challenges Ella faced in her youth helped her create music that was filled with emotion and heart. Her career as a singer spanned decades as Ella performed for sold-out audiences around the world and recorded more than 200 albums. Ella's impact on the world was more than just musical, though. Her talent and fame played a powerful role in bringing attention to the discrimination that people of color, including Ella, faced throughout the United States. Ella died in 1996 at age seventy-nine, but her music—and her inspiring legacy—lives on.

Benjamin Franklin was a man of many talents. He was born on January 17, 1706, in Boston, decades before the thirteen colonies would declare their independence from England—with significant help from him. Despite his keen curiosity and impressive intellect, Ben left school at age ten. He eventually secured an apprenticeship at a print shop, which was a perfect position for someone with such a gift with words. Ben wrote everything from anonymous advice columns to political pamphlets to weather reports. Ben's flair for words led him to coin several clever sayings that we still use today (some of them are included in this book!).

As a Founding Father of the United States, Benjamin Franklin helped write the Declaration of Independence and the Constitution, two essential documents that have shaped the nation. He was never elected to the presidency, but Ben served the newly founded country in many other ways. He was even the first postmaster general, making sure that mail was successfully delivered throughout the original thirteen colonies.

In addition to his important roles as a Founding Father and a talented writer, Ben's natural curiosity led him to make important discoveries in science and math. He conducted a dangerous experiment by tying a key to a kite in the middle of a lightning storm, hoping to prove that lightning was a form of electricity. Ben was also responsible for many popular inventions, including bifocal glasses, rocking chairs, and swim fins. Though he died on April 17, 1790, Benjamin Franklin's contributions continue to impact our lives.

MEET RANGER

A time–traveling golden retriever with search-and-rescue training . . . and a nose for danger!

scholastic.com

RANGER7